Raves for *The Godstone by* Violette Malan

"Malan doles out the details of this fascinating world sparingly, keeping the reader engaged in the many mysteries, including why and how the level of technology seems to change as the travelers move through different Modes along the Road. Well-drawn characters and a quest that's eventually revealed to be as epic as they come add depth to the story, but the standout here is this strange, highly original world. . . . An original, enigmatic fantasy about reluctant heroes drawn into a quest to save the world."
—*Kirkus*

"Malan transports readers to an exciting world of high-stakes magic in this epic fantasy series launch. . . . Malan's elaborate worldbuilding and nuanced characters help keep the pages turning on the way to the slow-building climax. The unexpected plot twists and a subtle hint of romance will leave readers eagerly awaiting the next installment." —*Publishers Weekly*

"I like to think I have my own preferences nailed down, and then a totally original book like Violette Malan's *The Godstone* comes along and thoroughly delights and surprises me. . . . There's a confident briskness to Malan's pacing; nothing seems to drag over *The Godstone*'s 300 or so pages. The momentum is only aided by the superb dialogue throughout. Fenra and Arlyn's banter is so pleasant, so assured, that it at times reads like classic English literature. Readers would be wise to pick up this exciting start to a new fantasy series." —BookPage

"Come for the characters and themes, stay for the plotting and worldbuilding, or the reverse. I loved it." —Nerds of a Feather

"I couldn't put it down! . . . *The Godstone* was a satisfying, self contained fantasy with just enough weird to pull you in and keep things fresh." —Powder & Page

"*The Godstone* is an adventure story. And a quest. And a story about being forced to dismantle a comfortable persona in order to do what desperately needs to be done. Which just so happens to turn out to be saving the world." —Reading Reality

**DAW Books proudly presents
the novels of Violette Malan**

THE GODSTONE
THE COURT WAR*

The Mirror Lands
THE MIRROR PRINCE
SHADOWLANDS

The Novels of Dhulyn and Parno
THE SLEEPING GOD
THE SOLDIER KING
THE STORM WITCH
PATH OF THE SUN

*Coming soon from DAW Books